I'll never let you go

WRITTEN AND ILLUSTRATED BY

Marianne Richmond

sourcebooks
jabberwocky

Published by Sourcebooks Jabberwocky, an imprint of Sourcebooks, Inc.
P.O. Box 4410, Naperville, Illinois 60567-4410
(630) 961-3900
Fax: (630) 961-2168
www.jabberwockykids.com

Source of Production: Leo Paper, Heshan City, China
Date of Production: December 2013
Run Number: 21654

Printed and bound in China.
LEO 10 9 8 7 6 5 4 3 2 1

Dedicated to Carl, Buddy, Ellie, and Timothy, who are forever part of our family.

Edward and Blankie met on
the first day of Edward.

From that day forward,
they were the BEST of friends...

And
always
together.

On walks
in the park.

During naptime.

Through
thunderstorms.

In the
doctor's office.

And tucked in **cozy** at bedtime.

"I'll never let you go,"

said Edward to Blankie.

It's true that Blankie would
do **anything** for Edward.

Be the *table* for his picnic.

The roof of his fort.

Or the **cape** for his magician costume.

"I'll never let you go!" said Edward to Blankie.

Even when Edward
went on vacation,
he took Blankie along.

To play on the beach.

Ride go-carts.

Or to toast marshmallows
under the stars.

One time, Blankie almost stayed in Florida
when Edward left him at the Spaghetti Shack.

The waitress **RAN**
out to the parking lot.

Thank You!!

"I'll never let you go,"
said Edward,

and he put Blankie in his monkey backpack
for **extra** safe keeping.

They took care of each other in other ways, too.

Blankie dried Edward's tears when he was sad.

Edward and Mama gave Blankie
a bath when he had **too many**
orange popsicle stains on him.

WASH. DRY.
REPEAT

STAIN
AWAY

Edward sat and waited in front of the dryer.

"I miss you," he said
as Blankie went round and round.

"This is good practice for when you go to school," said Mama.

"What is?"

"Being without Blankie for awhile."

"Oh no," said Edward.

"I'll never let him go."

School began after summer,
when the leaves started to turn orange.

"Why can't Blankie come to
school with me?" asked Edward.

"Because," said Mama.
"School is a GREAT place
to make new friends and
try new things. It's a fun
part of growing up."

"Hmph," Edward grumbled.
"He'll be sad," Edward said and covered Blankie
so he couldn't hear their talking.

"It's like me and you," said Mama.

"I'll be sad without you, too, but more
happy about your new school adventure!"

"Can we give Blankie some new
things to do, too, so he doesn't
miss me so much?" asked Edward.

They made a list.

"Play with my stuffed animals," said Edward.

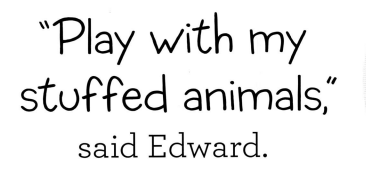

"*Swing* on the clothesline," said Mama.

"Take a nap with kitty,"
added Edward.

"*Help* me in the garden,"
said Mama.

"WOW, he'll be busy!"
laughed Edward.

"Will Blankie know I still love him even when we're apart?" asked Edward.

"Do you know *I* still love you even when we're apart?" asked Mama.

"Yes," said Edward.

"Then *he* will, too."

Mama tucked the two under the covers.

"When you love someone, you're always together in **here**," she said, patting her heart.

Edward and Blankie liked that answer.

"Is that where I'll be when I'm at school?" asked Edward, putting his hand over Mama's.

"Yes, forever and always," said Mama.

"No matter where you are.

No matter how big you grow.

My heart will **never**,
                    EVER, let you go."

About the Author

Beloved author and illustrator Marianne Richmond has touched the lives of millions for nearly two decades through her award-winning books and gift products that offer meaningful ways to connect with the people and moments that matter.